HOPE FLIES HIGH

Shannon Haywood

Illustrated by Anastasiia Ivshina

DEDICATION

For my husband Matt, the one I love the most, the one who always believes in me. I will love you forever!

PREFACE

American lives were forever changed on the beautiful morning of Tuesday, September 11, 2001. Hijackers, known as Al Qaeda, decided to take over airplane flights with the goal of taking as many American lives as possible.

At 8:46 am, in New York, American Airlines Flight 11 hit the north tower of the buildings known as the World Trade Center. Then, seventeen minutes later, a second plane crashed into the south tower. Simultaneously, in Washington D.C. American Airlines 77 slammed into the Pentagon, a US government building that is the head of the US Department of Defense. Then another crash occurred in Shanksville, Pennsylvania (as hero passengers tried to regain control of the hijacked plane) and diverted the plane to crash into a field instead of another building, taking even more innocent lives.

Our world was filled with smoke, chaos, death, destruction, and unanswered questions. However, during this war-like time, the people of the UNITED STATES OF AMERICA came together to save people from the rubbish and debris that fell from the sky. Police, fire, rescue, old, young, and everyone in between rose to the occasion to do what needed to be done... help one another. From this day, heroes came in all shapes and sizes.

That's a brief history lesson you may need to understand this story I will tell you. This story is about one unsung hero that I watched. This heroine quietly did what she thought she needed to do. She needed to show the people of New York and other places a way never to lose hope. She did not run into burning buildings or perform miraculous, life-saving surgeries.

This heroine is my mom, who gave hope to those who most needed it.

My mom and I lived in New York when the attacks happened. We had to evacuate the area immediately and return later when it was safe.

Since the plane crashes were as if multiple bombs exploded all at once, and even though we lived on the other side of town from the World Trade Center crash sites we had to make sure our building was not damaged.

My Mom and I patiently waited until residents in our neighborhood could return.

We lived two bus rides away from the actual Twin Towers; smoke, ash, charred bits of buildings, crushed car parts, shattered glass, crumbles of bricks, and layers of debris were what was now paving the way to the neighborhood, in which mom and I lived.

In New York, Mom and I were used to walking everywhere. We walked to parks and school, and Mom walked to work and even the grocery store. We could get anywhere we needed in just a short walk.

However, walking down the corridor of the neighborhood was somber and disheartening. Home didn't seem like home anymore. But, even then, it was good to be home...weeks after the world stood still.

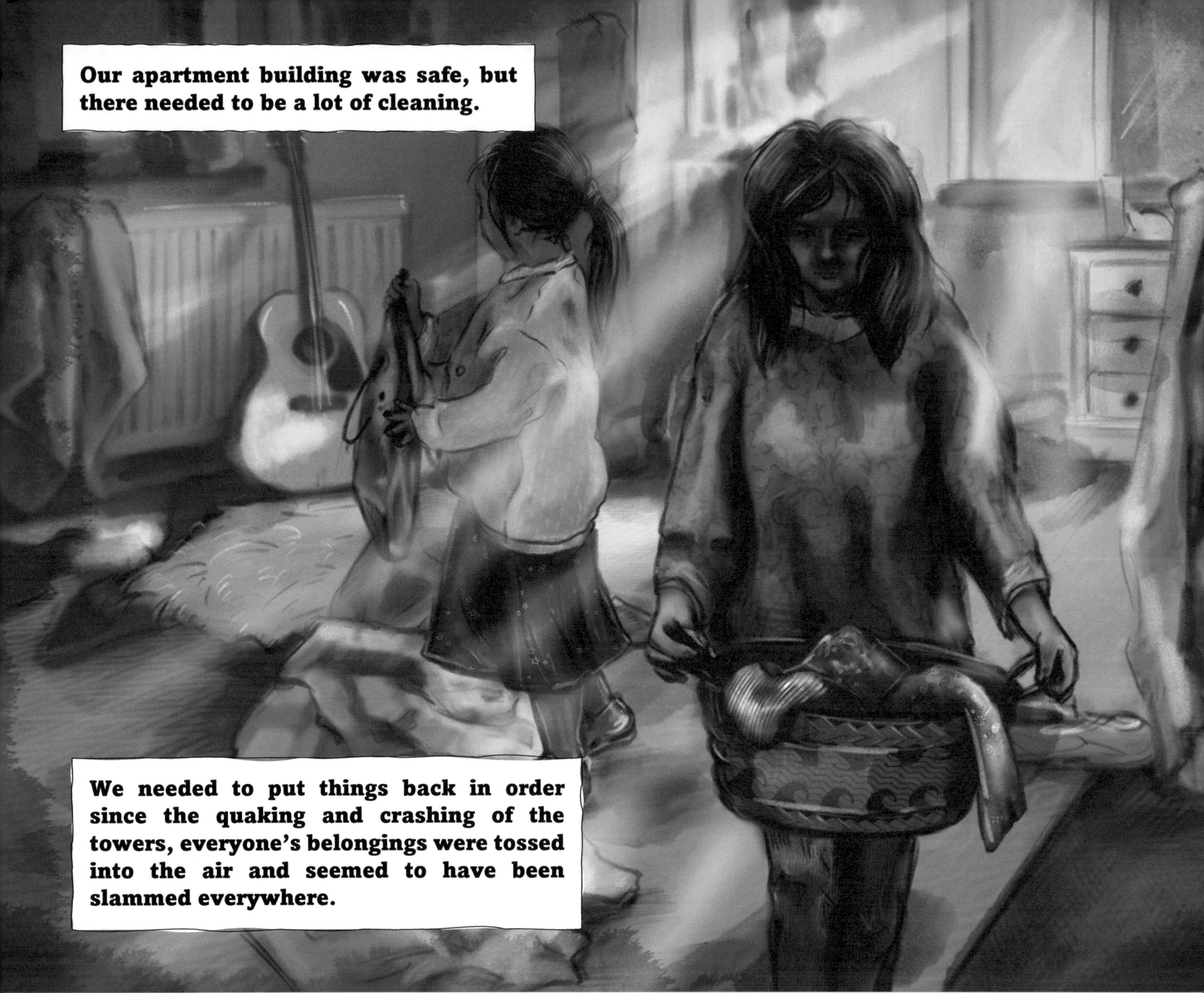
Our apartment building was safe, but there needed to be a lot of cleaning.
We needed to put things back in order since the quaking and crashing of the towers, everyone's belongings were tossed into the air and seemed to have been slammed everywhere.

On that dreadful day, many lives were lost, and a deep sadness draped across the nation. Even Mom and I had very few laughs and silly moments.

However, with the cape of sadness, I noticed people seemed to appreciate the little things in life. Food, water, kind words, and gestures were precious treasures. People needed hope - and that's how Mom became a hero.

As we started cleaning the apartment, it was evident that the world's colors had faded away. The surroundings looked dark, lifeless, and gray. However, Mom and I continued dusting and cleaning and gradually noticed small hints of color emerging from the clutter.

While taking a lunch break, Mom and I decided to eat outside, the air was clear and crisp, and it felt good to be home.

After eating our sandwiches, Mom and I strolled through the area. We saw everyone working to find a new normal for their home. The color seemed to fade away once again.

Suddenly, mom gasped and walked briskly across the street while I watched, wondering, "What is she doing?" She got down on her hands and knees and reached her hand into the disgusting grates of the storm drain. I could not believe what I was seeing. I thought, "What could be so important that you would put your arms elbow-deep in one of the grossest places on a New York street?"

Mom sat deliberately back on the curb. It seemed like I was watching a video in super slow motion. She gently pulled something from the drain. I couldn't even tell what it was...maybe some sort of cloth or sheet. And then, Mom clinched it to her chest, the absolute most repulsive looking, nauseating-smelling piece of garbage I ever saw.

Mom's eyes had soaked into the filthy cloth, and I realized the tears were not tears of despair but of promise, dreams, and resilience—tears of hope.

The tear-soaked cloth revealed the brightest, sharpest color of red I have ever witnessed in all the gray and dullness. I knew at that moment, Mom, in a heroic fashion, reached into the dark unknown to save an American flag from the bowels of the drain.

Mom rushed up and grabbed my hand. We raced back to the apartment, things were beginning to be restored, but we had a long way to go. All those other tasks were put on hold. Mom had to complete the rescue of hope.

Mom laid the flag on the kitchen table like a delicate flower. She grabbed the soap and made a pan of warm water. She searched the back of the bathroom drawer and found a toothbrush we had never opened.

She brought in a few towels and laid them on the floor in the rays of sunshine that beamed through the kitchen windows.

She and I got on our knees and began to brush the crust, dust, and dinge so lightly from the Stars and Stripes.
Mom would put the toothbrush into the warm, soapy water, and she would gently scrub each and every star.

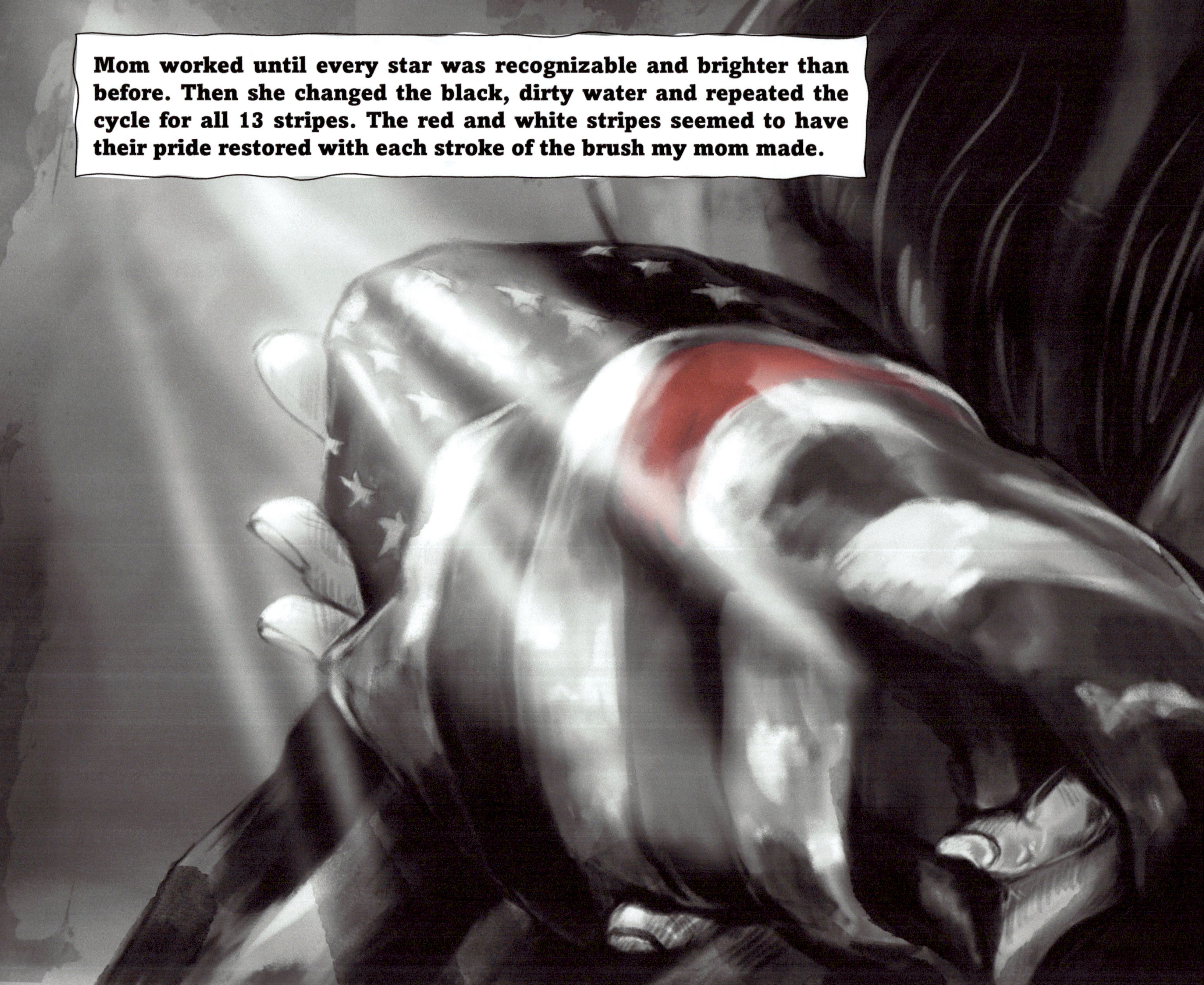

Mom worked until every star was recognizable and brighter than before. Then she changed the black, dirty water and repeated the cycle for all 13 stripes. The red and white stripes seemed to have their pride restored with each stroke of the brush my mom made.

The smell no longer encased the room, and the grit from the flag was being washed away. I sat and studied every move Mom made. She was purposeful and proud. She scrubbed the tattered, ragged flag for hours until...finally, she stepped back, and there an image of honor...Old Glory lay before us. The flag was majestic and radiated with hope for all. Mom cried again. I shed some tears of joy too.

Before the 9/11 tragedy, our apartment building always had an empty flagpole. So, Mom and I knew exactly what to do with the flag. We folded the flag until the three corners were tight. Mom had one hand on top and one on the bottom of the folded flag. We walked to the front garden area of our building. Our neighbors saw what we were carrying and followed us out. Mom led me to the pole and taught me how to raise the flag carefully and honorably.

Our neighbors gathered around the flagpole; tears silently fell from every eye. Mom and I placed our hands over our hearts, and there, the entire neighborhood stood tall and, in unison, repeated the best version of the Pledge of Allegiance that had ever been promised.

Hope was restored.

My mom was the neighborhood hero. She saved the flag. The United States of America Flag was flying high again. The red was faded, the white was dingy, the blue was stained, and the ends were frayed, but it was the most colorful and vivid symbol of hope and freedom that I ever saw. My mom did that!

ABOUT THE AUTHOR

I am Shannon Haywood. I was born and raised in Rockingham, North Carolina. I have been an educator in a public-school setting for 24 years. I have presented at reading conferences and led professional development sessions for teachers across various grade and content levels.

As an educator, I learned early in my career to examine children's picture books with a purpose. Picture books can teach perspective, themes, support inferences, and questions built in a reader's mind. The text of picture books have enriching vocabulary and language that will support and foster engaging thoughts of the reader. That is what I want for all readers and teachers.

Use this picture book, *Hope Flies High*, to discover all the hidden lessons between the pages. Life's lessons can be learned by one picture book at a time.